PEARL HARBOR

Amy Culliford

TABLE OF CONTENTS

A Pelican Book

SEAHORSE
PUBLISHING

Teaching Tips for Caregivers and Teachers:

Research shows that one of the best ways for students to learn a new topic is to read about it.

Before Reading

- Read the title and predict what the book will be about.
- Read the "Words to Know" and discuss the meaning of each word.
- Read the back cover to see what the book is about.

During Reading

- When a student gets to a word that is unknown, ask them to look at the rest of the sentence to find clues to help with the meaning of the unknown word.
- Motivate students with praise and encouragement.

After Reading

- Discuss the main idea of the book.
- Ask students to give one detail that they learned in the book.

Sight Words

a	I	see
big	in	there
day	is	to
each	it	was
go	many	
here	people	

Words to Know

 **battle**

 **battleship**

 **Hawaii**

 **museum**

 **Pearl Harbor**

3

I see **Pearl Harbor!**

4

Pearl Harbor

Pearl Harbor is in **Hawaii**.

UNITED STATES OF AMERICA

WASHINGTON
OREGON
IDAHO
MONTANA
NORTH DAKOTA
MINNESOTA
WISCONSIN
MICHIGAN
VERMONT
MAINE
NEW HAMPSHIRE
MASSACHUSETTS
NEW YORK
RHODE ISLAND
CONNECTICUT
NEVADA
WYOMING
SOUTH DAKOTA
IOWA
PENNSYLVANIA
NEW JERSEY
UTAH
NEBRASKA
ILLINOIS
INDIANA
OHIO
MARYLAND
DELAWARE
CALIFORNIA
COLORADO
KANSAS
MISSOURI
KENTUCKY
WEST VIRGINIA
VIRGINIA
ARIZONA
NEW MEXICO
OKLAHOMA
ARKANSAS
TENNESSEE
NORTH CAROLINA
SOUTH CAROLINA
TEXAS
MISSISSIPPI
ALABAMA
GEORGIA
LOUISIANA
FLORIDA

Hawaii

ALASKA

HAWAII

It is a **museum**.

museum

There was a big **battle** here.

battle

There is a **battleship**!

battleship

Many people go to see Pearl Harbor each day!

Index

Written by: Amy Culliford

Design by: Under the Oaks Media

Series Development: James Earley

Editor: Kim Thompson

Photos: SvetlanaSF: cover; Mayskyphoto: p. 3,5; PomlnOz: p. 3,9; U.S Naval History and Heritage Command Photograph: p. 3,11; Phillip Kraskoff: p. 3,13; Studio Barcelona: p. 3,15

Library of Congress PCN Data

Pearl Harbor / Amy Culliford

U.S. Landmarks

ISBN 978-1-6389-7959-3 (hard cover)

ISBN 979-8-8873-5018-9 (paperback)

ISBN 979-8-8873-5077-6 (EPUB)

ISBN 979-8-8873-5136-0 (eBook)

Library of Congress Control Number: 2022943688

Printed in the United States of America.

Seahorse Publishing Company

seahorsepub.com

Published in the United States
Seahorse Publishing
PO Box 771325
Coral Springs, FL 33077